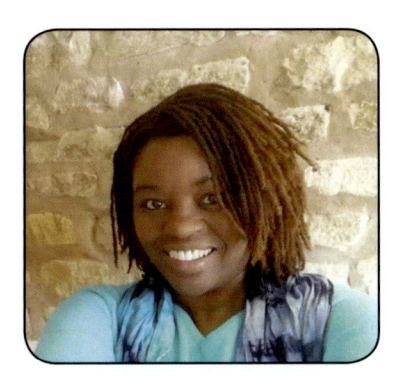

Fadzisai Gukuta (nee Musa) is a pharmacist by profession and also a singer/songwriter, simply *Shamiso*. She now adds being an author to her growing list of credentials as she debuts this illustrated offering. Born and raised in the picturesque Zimbabwe, she writes mainly in English but seasons her work with sprinklings of her native language, Shona. She has lived in Birmingham, UK, for most of her adult life.

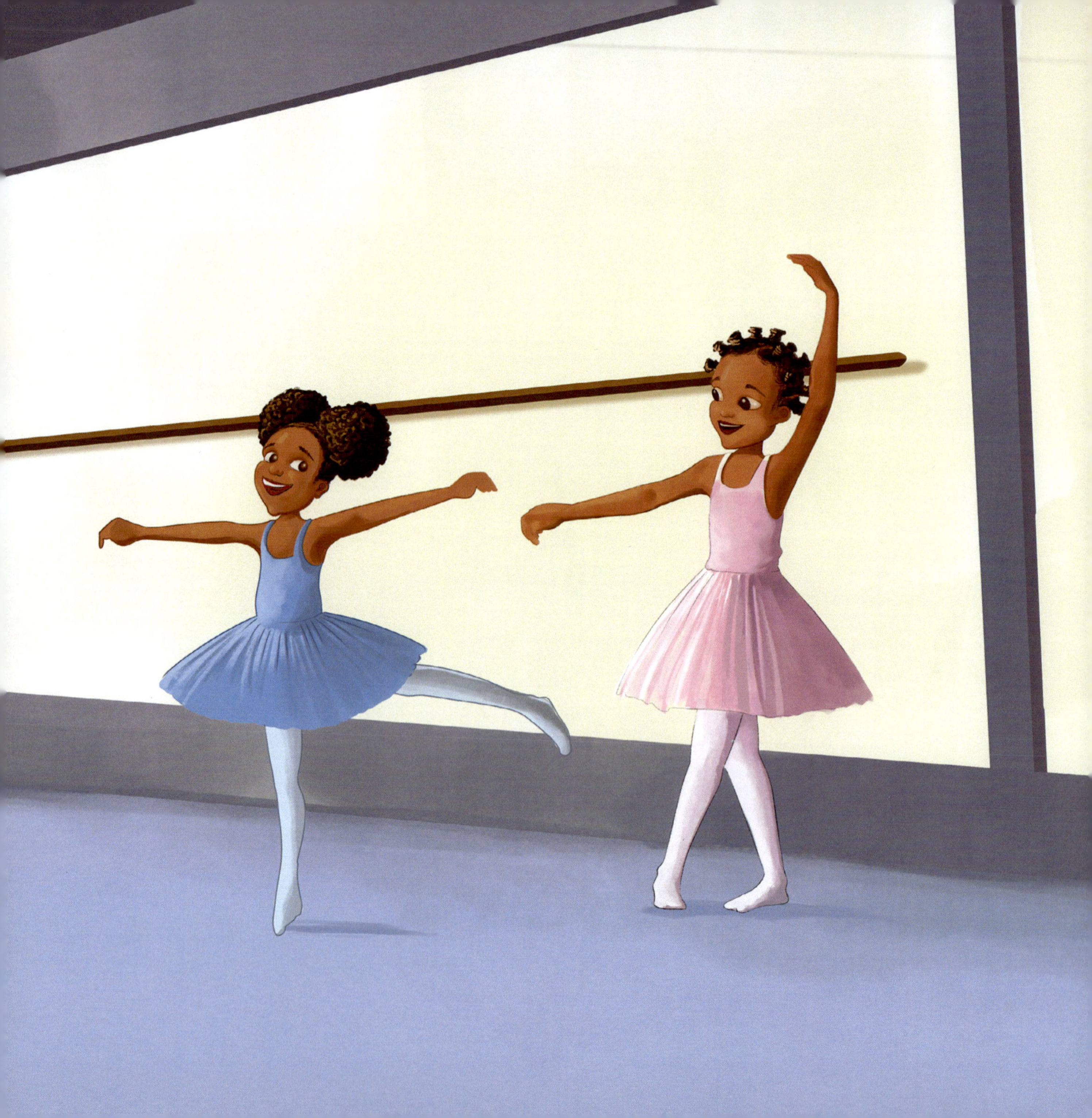

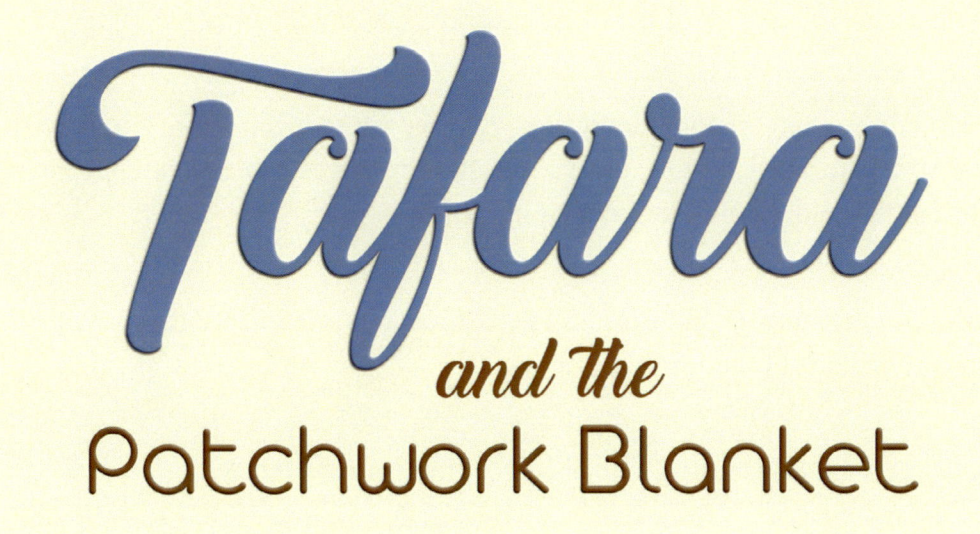

FADZISAI GUKUTA

Tafara
and the Patchwork Blanket

AUSTIN MACAULEY PUBLISHERS
LONDON • CAMBRIDGE • NEW YORK • SHARJAH

Copyright © Fadzisai Gukuta (2020)

The right of **Fadzisai Gukuta** to be identified as author of this work has been asserted by her in accordance with section 77 and 78 of the Copyright, Designs and Patents Act 1988.

All rights reserved. No part of this publication may be reproduced, stored in a retrieval system, or transmitted in any form or by any means, electronic, mechanical, photocopying, recording, or otherwise, without the prior permission of the publishers.

Any person who commits any unauthorised act in relation to this publication may be liable to criminal prosecution and civil claims for damages.

A CIP catalogue record for this title is available from the British Library.

ISBN 9781528906753 (Paperback)
ISBN 9781528958370 (ePub e-book)

www.austinmacauley.com

First Published (2020)
Austin Macauley Publishers Ltd
25 Canada Square
Canary Wharf
London
E14 5LQ

Dedication

I would like to dedicate this book to my daughters, Ashlyn and Yananiso Gukuta. I would like them to grow up in a world where nothing stops them and other children from reaching their full potential. I also take great pleasure in dedicating this book to my nephew, Tonderai Michael Sanyangore, a distinguished gentleman who was born with and suffers from albinism. He has a fantastic sense of humour and a great work ethic, and is an exemplary human being.

Acknowledgements

I'd like to thank Rhoda Molife of Molah Media for her encouragement and support in bringing this book to life. She also did the first edit of the book. My thanks go to Mussah Mupfurutsa for suggesting I write a book in the first place. The two aforementioned ladies are my sisters, and I'm so proud to be associated with women who uplift others so much. I thank Tonderai Michael Sanyangore for his insights into life as an albinism-sufferer. I draw on inspiration from real-life conversations so for this I thank my family – my parents, David and Constance Musa; my daughters, Ashlyn and Yananiso; and my husband, George. George is eternally patient and long-suffering as he gives me time and grace to explore and nurture my dreams, and to him I am truly grateful. I thank God for the insights and revelations He gives me and the ability to articulate them.

CONTENTS

Chapter 01 — 10

Chapter 02 — 12

Chapter 03 — 22

Chapter 04 — 26

Chapter 05 — 34

Glossary — 38

Author's Note — 39

Chapter 01

Tafara loved Saturdays.

It was the unpredictability she enjoyed, after the time-tabled bits, that is. There was her ballet lesson with Miss Katie. *First position, second position, third position, fourth. Lift your chins. Backs straight. Point your toes.*

Then as if on autopilot, she'd hop into her car seat when her lesson was finished and sing along at the top of her voice to the Moana Disney soundtrack, while *Baba*, her dad, drove her and her 5-year-old sister, Tanaka, to their swimming lesson. *Front crawl. Back stroke. Stretch those arms out. Kick those feet.*

Tafara and Tanaka were really lucky to live right next door to their grandparents. So, almost every Saturday, after all the time-tabled bits, they got to spend the day with *Gogo*, their grandmother. This is when the fun began. *Gogo* did all these wonderful things, and sometimes she would let 'her girls' – that's what she called them, 'my girls' – join in on whatever wonderful thing she was up to that day.

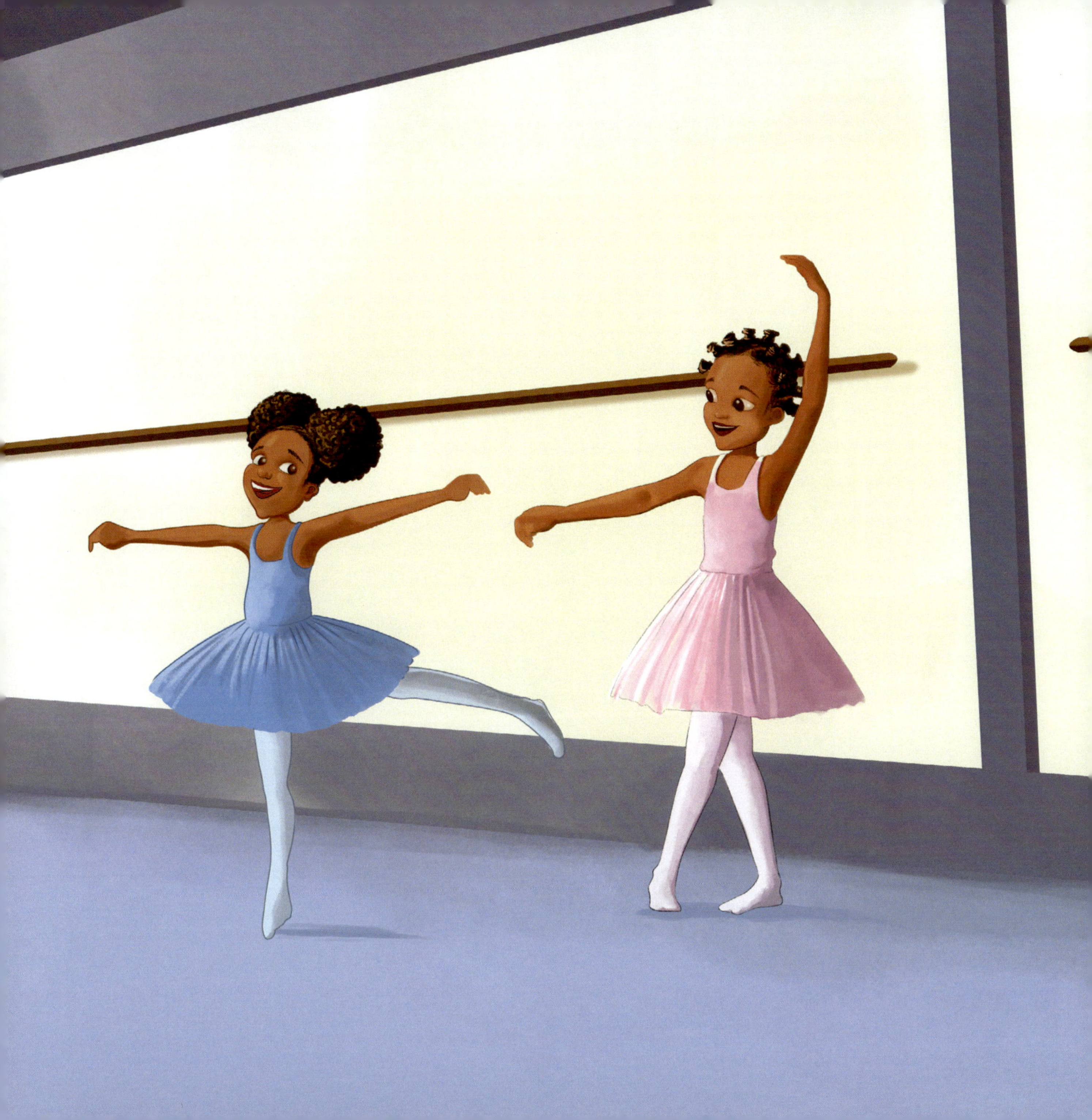

Chapter 02

On this Saturday, like all Saturdays, Tafara and Tanaka ran straight from the car into their grandparents' house, leaving *Baba* to trail behind them. He, as always, made sure they were safely indoors, before he walked next door to their house.

Today, *Gogo* was busily working away at her desk in a corner of the dining room. Tafara was thrilled to hear the *grrrr-grrrr-grrrr* of the sewing machine as it hummed and hemmed. A long time ago, when she was 2 years old, she had crawled under the table and pressed the foot pedal with her hand, making the machine go crazy and stitch a seam before *Gogo* was ready! The scolding she got meant she never, ever did it again. *Gogo* laughs about that day a lot now. *Gogo* loves to laugh!

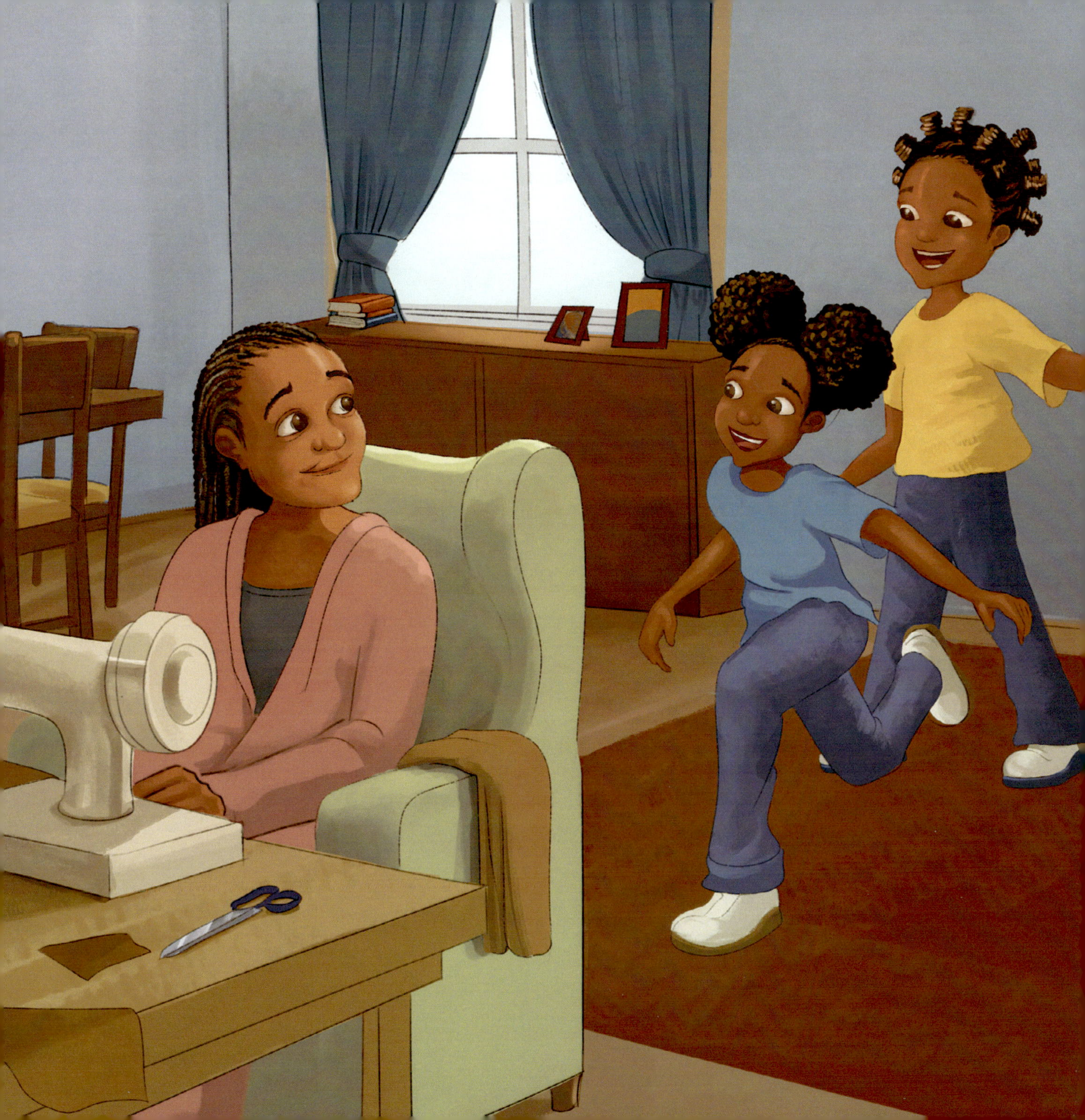

Anyway, scattered over the dining chairs was lots and lots of fabric, in every imaginable shade of cream and brown. Then Tafara and Tanaka saw it: square upon square sewn together in rows, and whatever it was that *Gogo* was making looked like it was nearly finished. They greeted her affectionately in their language.

"*Maswera sei, Gogo?*"

Before *Gogo* could answer, Tafara immediately asked, "*Chii chamurikugadzira, Gogo?*"

Tanaka chimed in without even knowing what *Gogo* was doing, "Can we help? Pleeeease?"

Gogo couldn't resist a chuckle. "Of course you can, my girls. I've been working on it every day while you've been at school, but I'm glad you get to see it now. It's coming along nicely. *Nd'a nda'akutopedza.*"

She stood up and shook out her creation so that they could get a better look. It was a blanket! Tafara and Tanaka shrieked. *Gogo* hushed them and reminded them that *Khulu*, their grandfather, was snoozing peacefully in the living room.

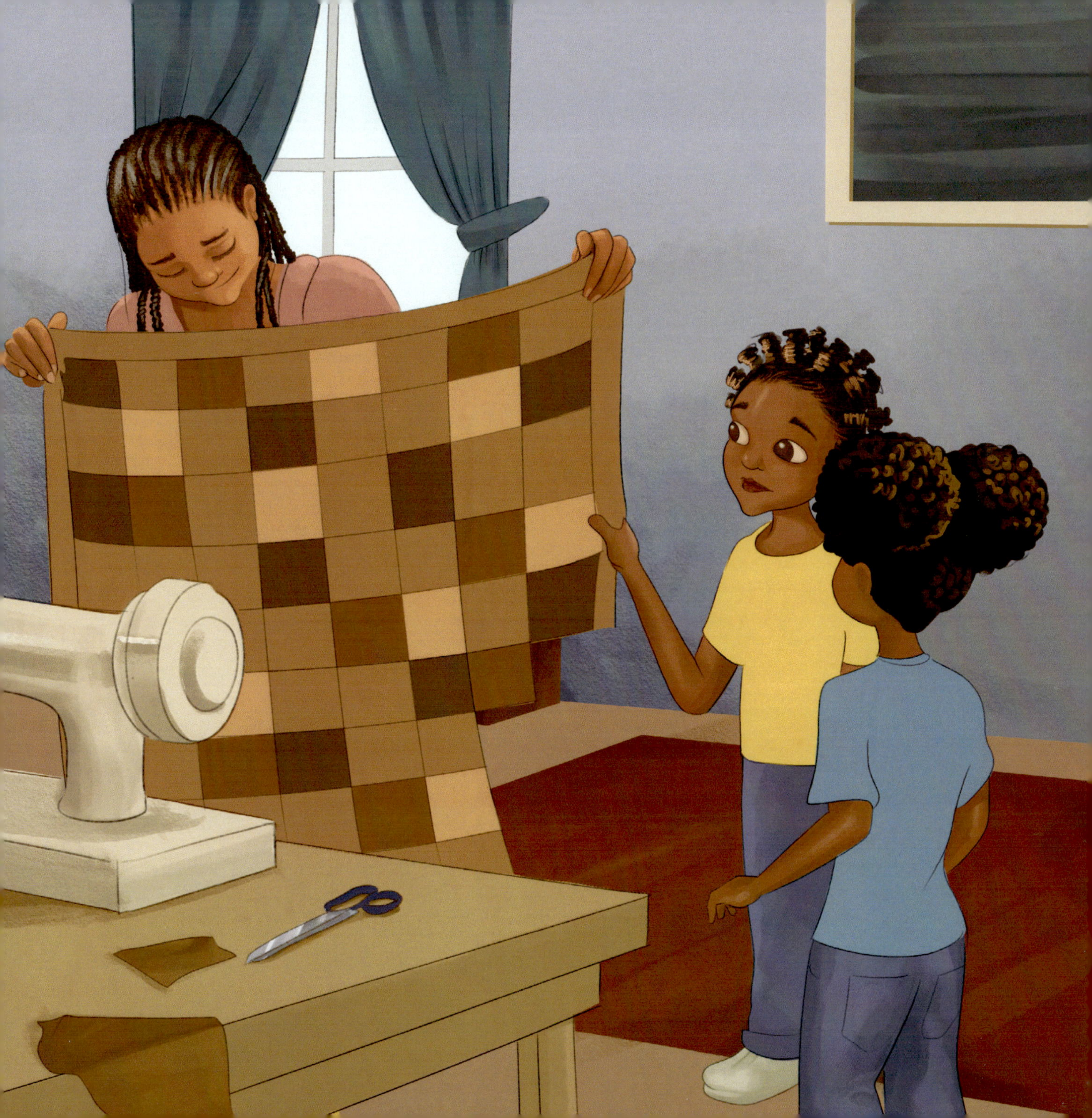

"I've got a few more rows to do, then it's done. What I need you to do, *vasikana*, is to choose some more scraps of fabric from that pile and help me add them here at the end."

Tafara and Tanaka dived into the piles of fabric, selected their favourites, then placed them on *Gogo's* square template. After tracing out some squares, they asked *Gogo* to carefully cut them out, after which she proceeded to masterfully stitch them to the nearly-finished blanket.

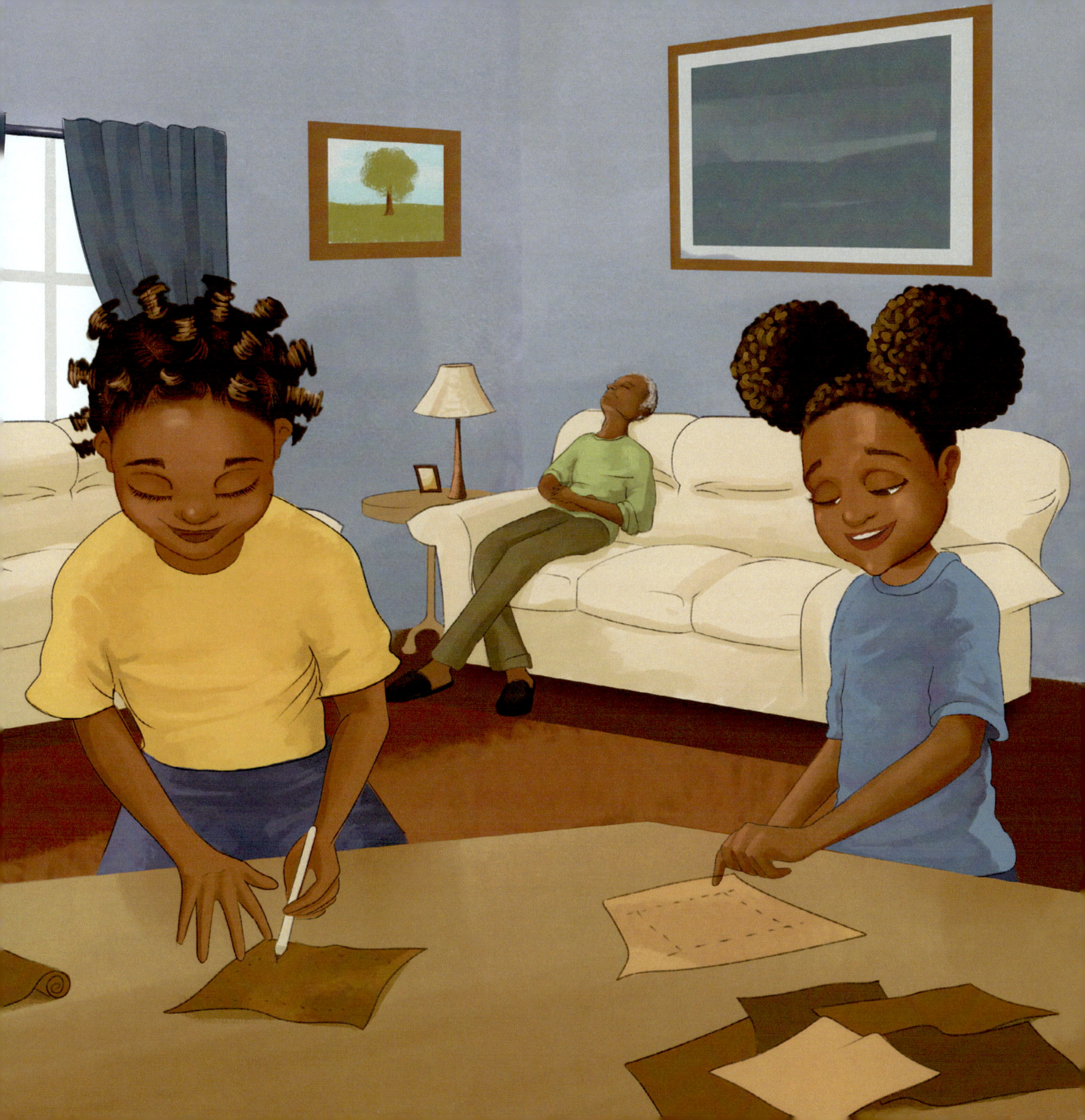

In the meantime, they took a break for a lunch of brown *sadza*, with kale and stewed beef. *Sadza* could be white as well, but their mum and dad preferred them to have wholesome versions of anything they could. Whatever they ate, if there was a brown alternative, they'd be sure to have it. They wolfed down the food and rushed back to *Gogo's* sewing corner. They then helped her cut long thin strips to neaten the outer edge of the blanket and by suppertime, it was all done.

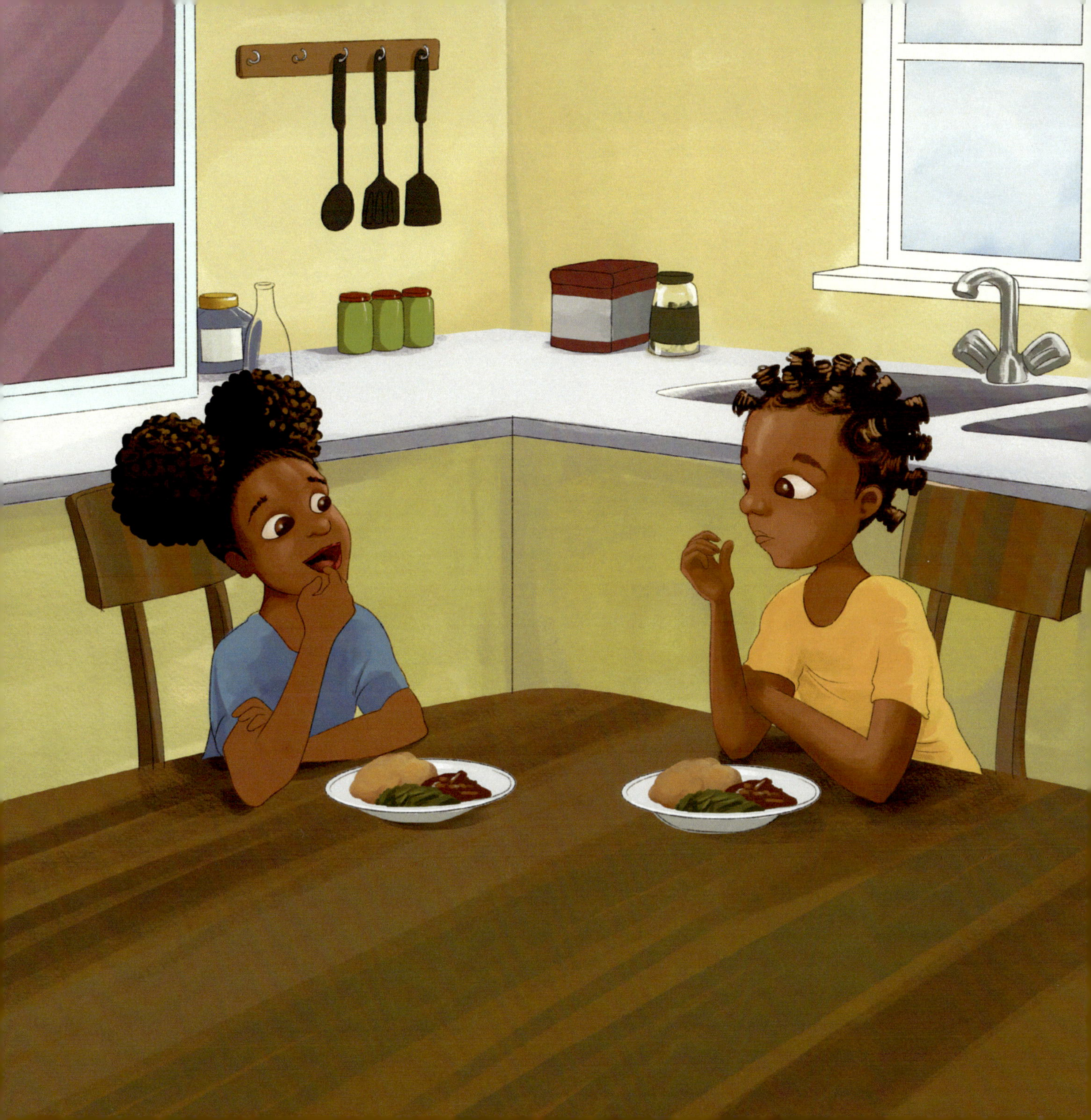

When Gogo held it up in all its splendour, the girls marvelled at her ingenuity! It was exquisite. She had expertly mixed different textures and shades of brown and lined the inside with fleece to make it extra warm. Gogo threw it around them and pulled them into a cosy embrace, tickling them as she did so. Her cuddles were as warm as her smile and made Tafara and Tanaka feel extra loved.

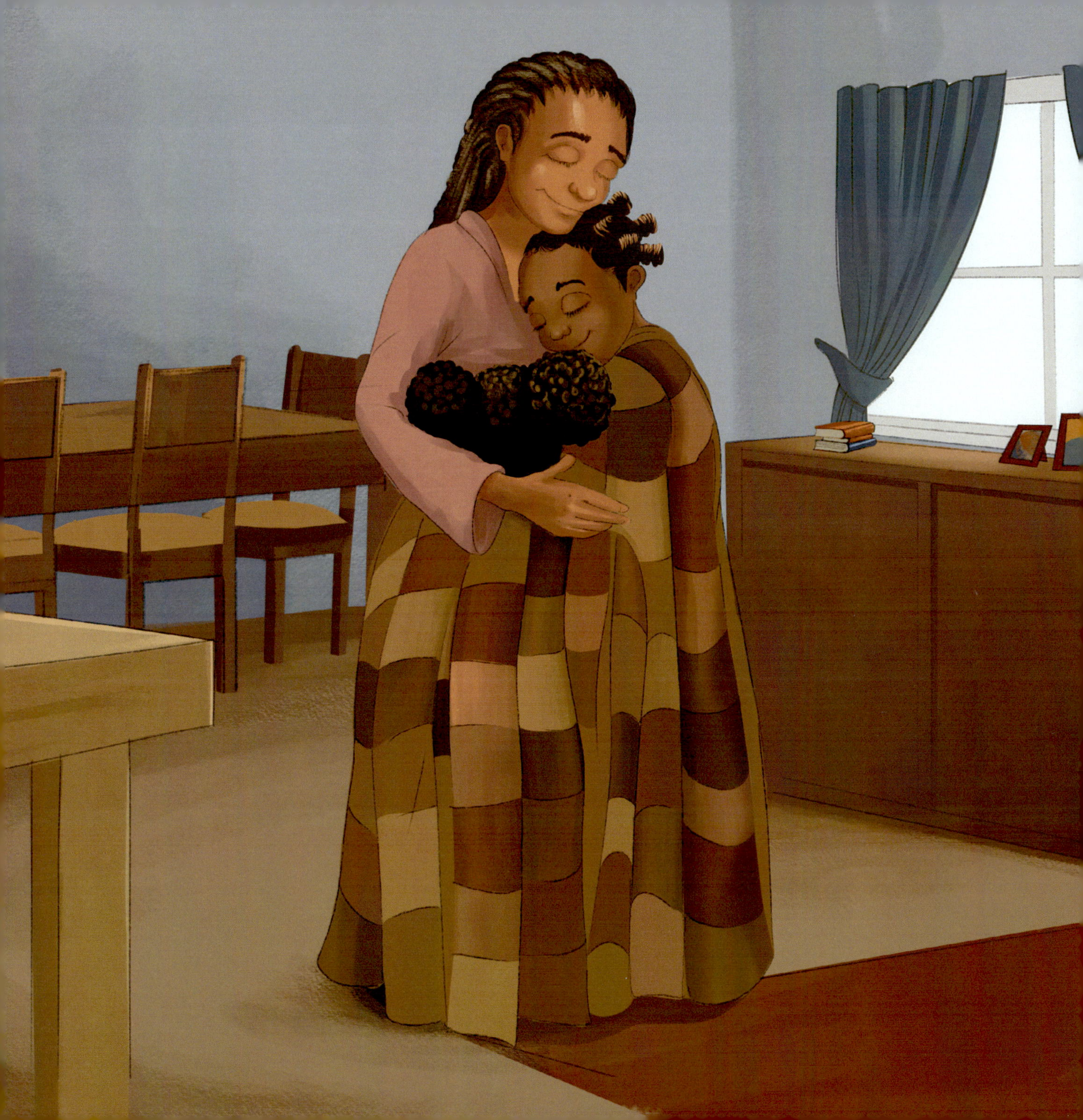

Chapter 03

Just then, Mama, their mother, joined them, having just got back from her job as a pharmacist. As Tafara and Tanaka leapt towards her, she scooped them up in her arms as they squealed in delight.

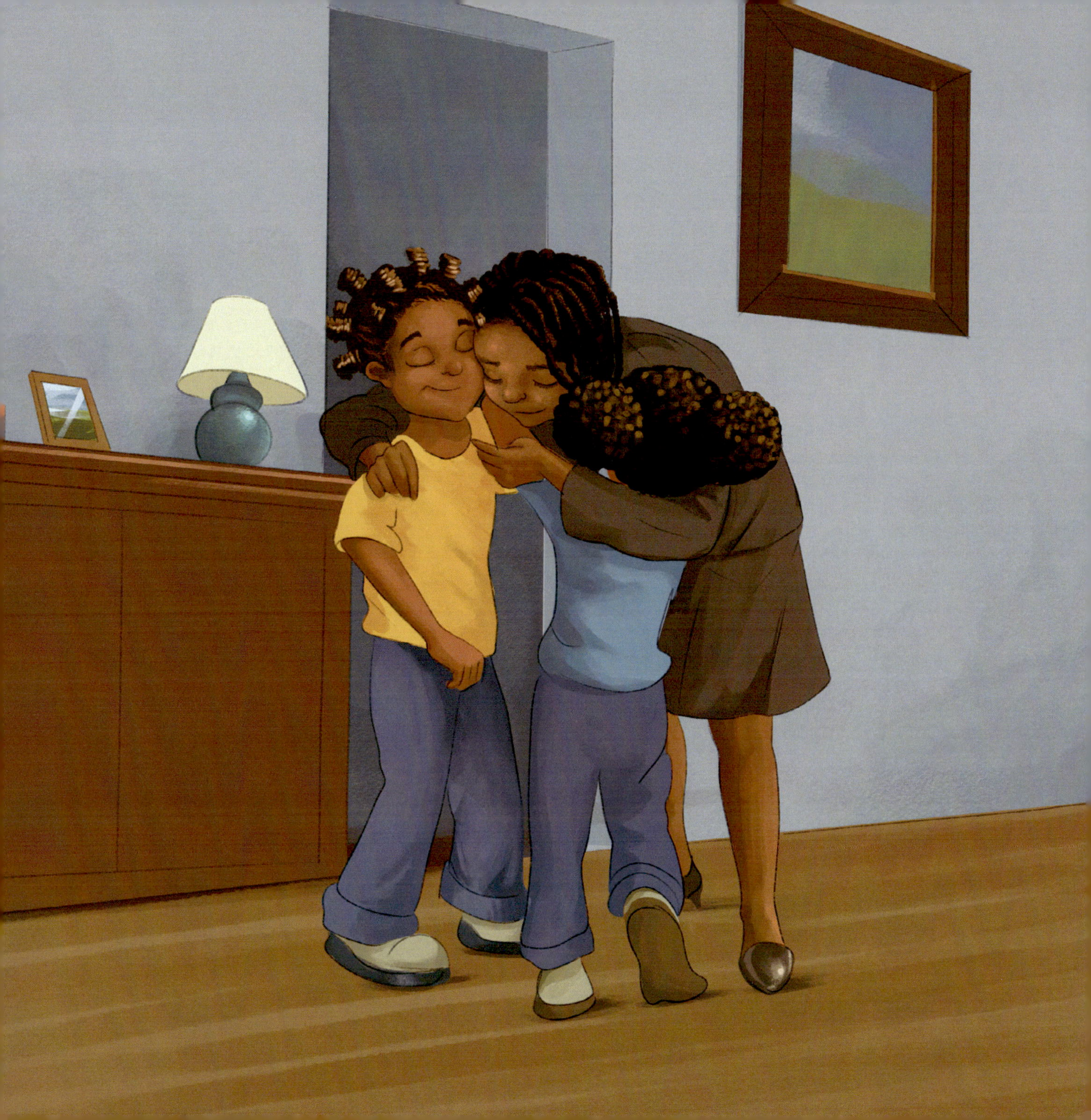

"*Maswera sei,* Mama?" they sang out in unison.

"*Ndaswera kanamaswerawo vasikana*?" she sang back.

"*Taswera*," they replied, without going into detail just yet about how magnificent their day was turning out to be.

Mama greeted *Gogo*, her mother, just as she had Tafara and Tanaka. She warmed herself some dinner before settling down to enjoy it in the big cream leather armchair near the sewing machine.

Out of the blue, Tafara piped up, "Mama, you know how brown food is better for us than white food…"

"*Ehe, mwan'angu*. It's less processed and brown *sadza* is made from *zviyo* and not *chibage*," she replied nonchalantly between mouthfuls.

"So, does that mean brown people are better than white people?" Tafara continued.

The forkful of food that was about to enter Mama's mouth had a sudden change of heart and slowly backed down onto her plate. Her bewildered expression showed she wasn't expecting this type of question. Her thoughts raced. *What? Why is an 8-year-old asking me this question? How did that thought even enter her head?* There was a pregnant pause as she grappled for the right answer, any answer, that wouldn't make Tafara feel silly for asking.

Then she saw the funny side and let out a chuckle.

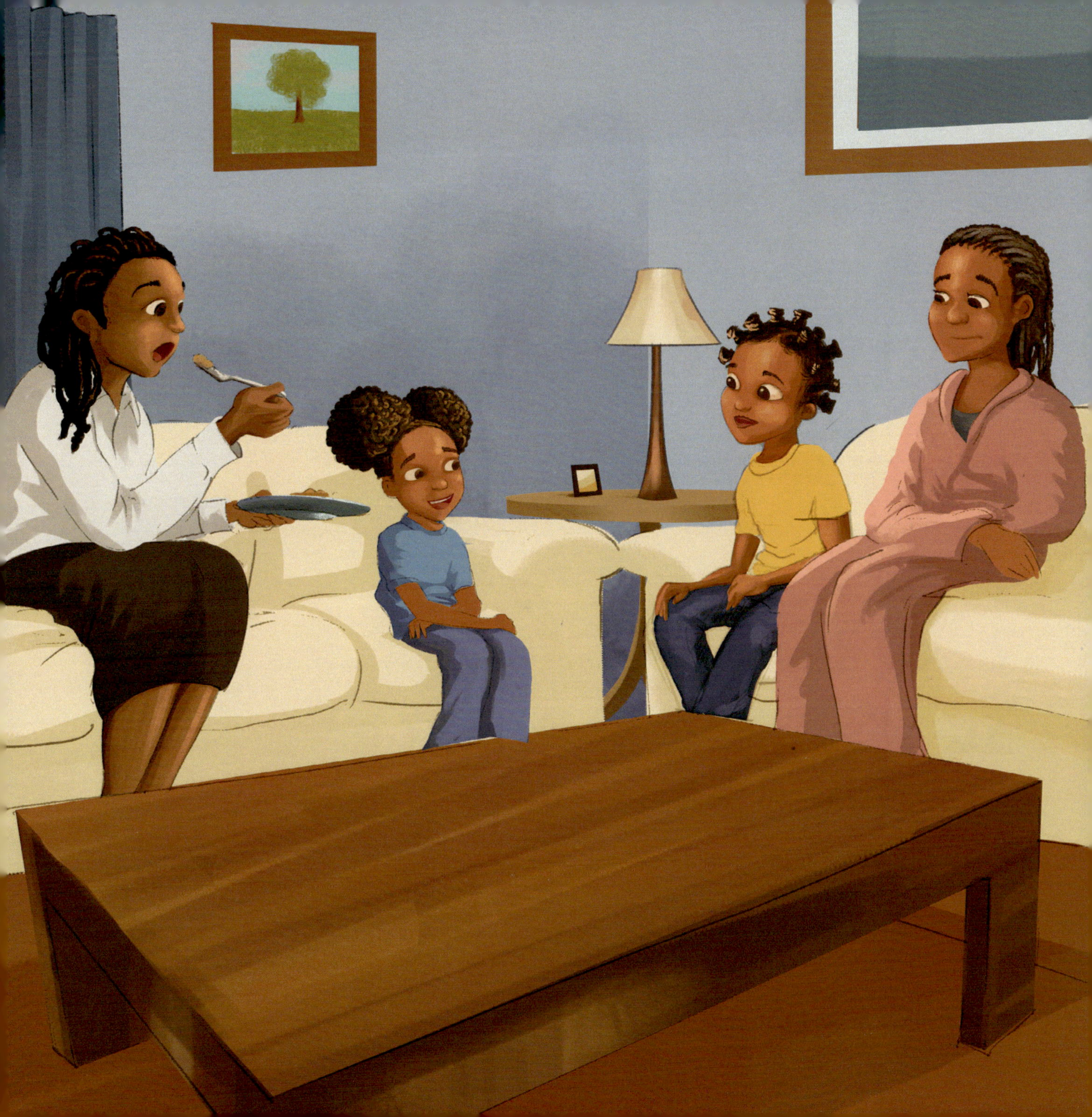

Chapter 04

Composing herself and clearing her throat, she replied, "No, sweetie. Your skin doesn't make you better or worse than anyone else. What matters is your character – being kind, considerate and respectful – and giving all that you do your very best shot. Make sure you aim to be the best person that you can be."

Just then, *Khulu* appeared out of nowhere. He was always ready to join a conversation where he could share his words of wisdom, even if he had just been in a deep sleep!

"Ah! *Mamuka*," *Gogo* remarked, chuckling at *Khulu*.

Khulu chuckled back, "*Ehe, ndamuka.*"

"Africans, well, brown people in general, have been responsible for many scientific breakthroughs and inventions in the past." *Khulu* never spared them the complexities of the English language. He totally disregarded their tender ages and spoke in meaty vocabulary, knowing full well that they'd ask the meanings of his words, which he'd take great delight in explaining at length.

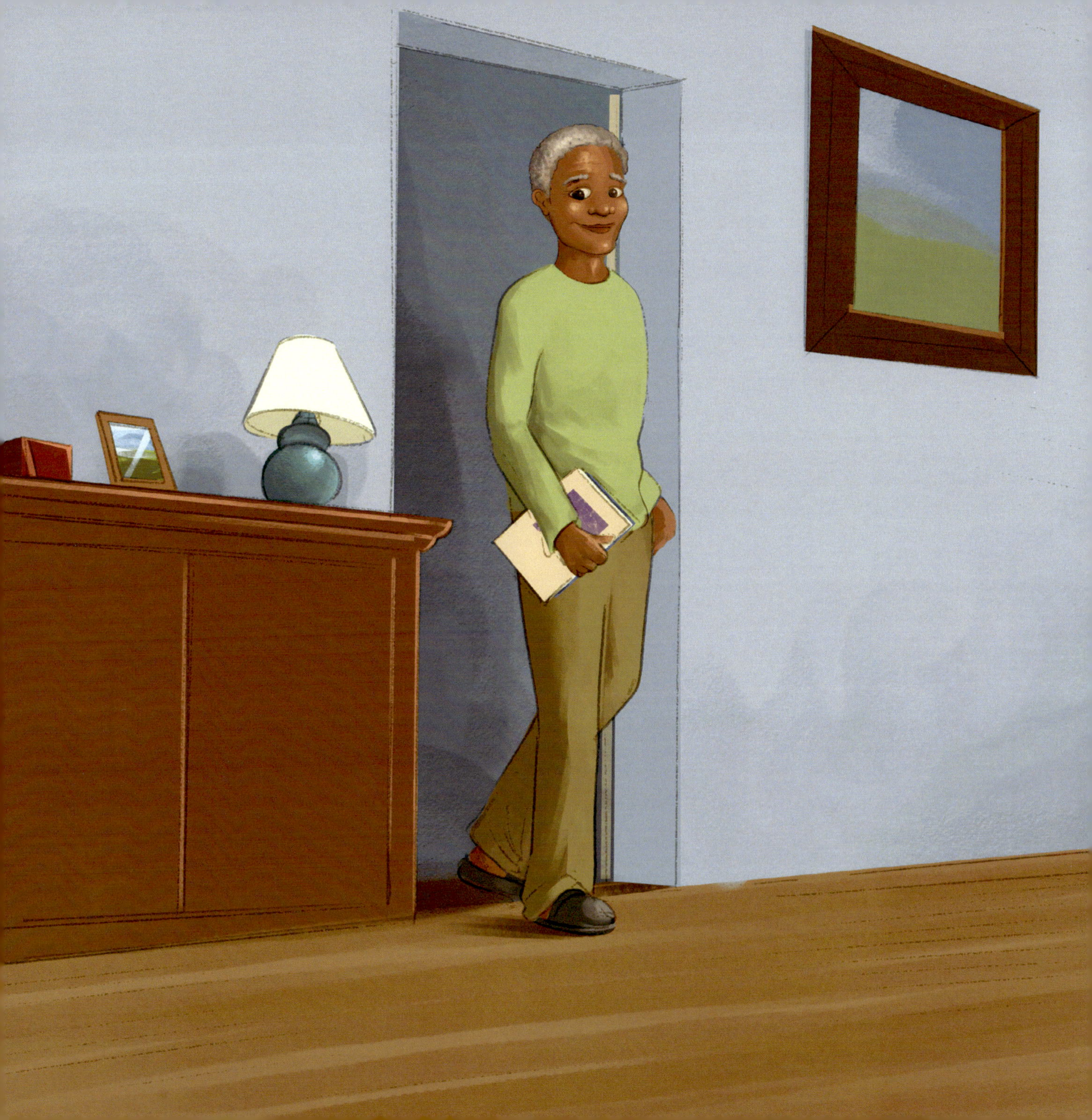

"Ah, *maswera*," Mama turned and greeted her father.

"*Taswera Mai* Tafara," replied *Khulu*. Greetings out of the way, *Khulu* continued, "They're intrinsically very intelligent..."

"And they're the best runners, like Usain Bolt!" Tanaka contributed, chuckling.

"Yes, Tanaka, and for anyone to be the best at what they do, they have to take their natural ability and nurture it. That means they must work very hard," *Khulu* said earnestly.

Gogo saw her opportunity, pulled the girls onto her lap and, with a glint in her eye, said, "Now, girls, you know what I love most about this blanket? It reminds me of all the different-coloured skin tones I see when I'm walking around in Birmingham. Dark ones, light ones and every shade in between. Why do you think human beings are different colours?"

Tanaka was pensive. "Because some of them haven't spent a long time in the sun?" she grinned, knowing her answer was ridiculous.

Gogo squeezed her and laughed graciously. "That's...interesting," she said. "What do you think, Tafara?"

"Well, I suppose it would be boring if everyone was the same," she stated confidently.

Gogo raised her right eyebrow, impressed by Tafara's answer. "True. You're absolutely right. Think of all the beautiful colours we see in autumn. What if the rainbow had only one colour? Or can you imagine if all those flowers in the garden were yellow? No violet ones, or blue ones, or red ones, or pink ones? And what if all your clothes were the same colour?"

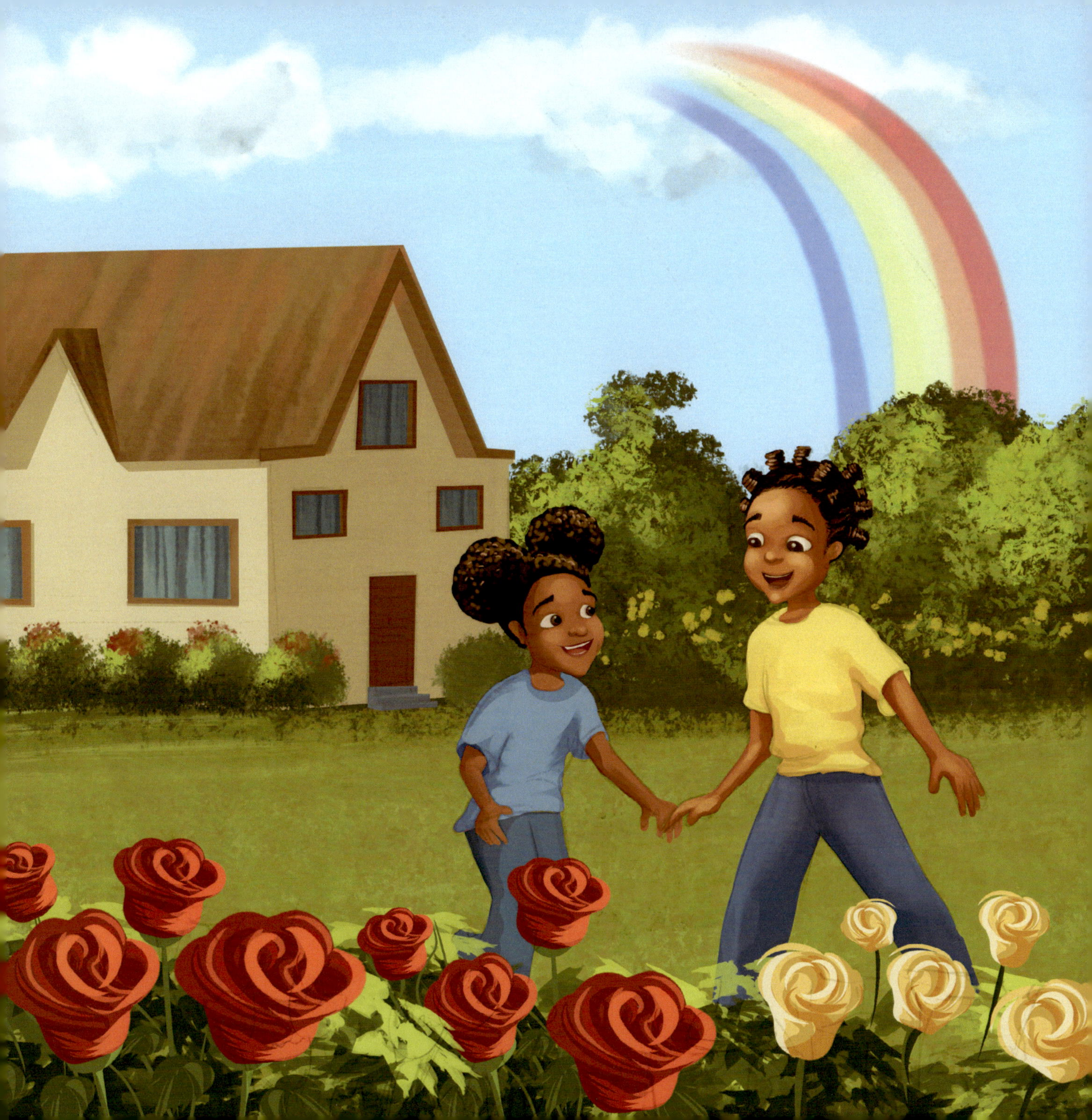

"Yup! That would be definitely dull!" confirmed Tanaka.

"But how come 'people' are different colours? How come I have black skin and my friend Poppy has white skin?" Tafara asked.

"Melanin" came a voice from the doorway. Tafara and Tanaka's dad, *Baba*, had overheard the conversation as he walked in through the front door, poking his head 'round just at the right time. He was a software engineer but knew everything about everything, not just computers! Tanaka and Tafara were confused.

"Remember when we were outside, and I was explaining that the leaves were green because of a pigment called chlorophyll?" he continued.

"Yeeees," Tafara replied, slowly and deliberately.

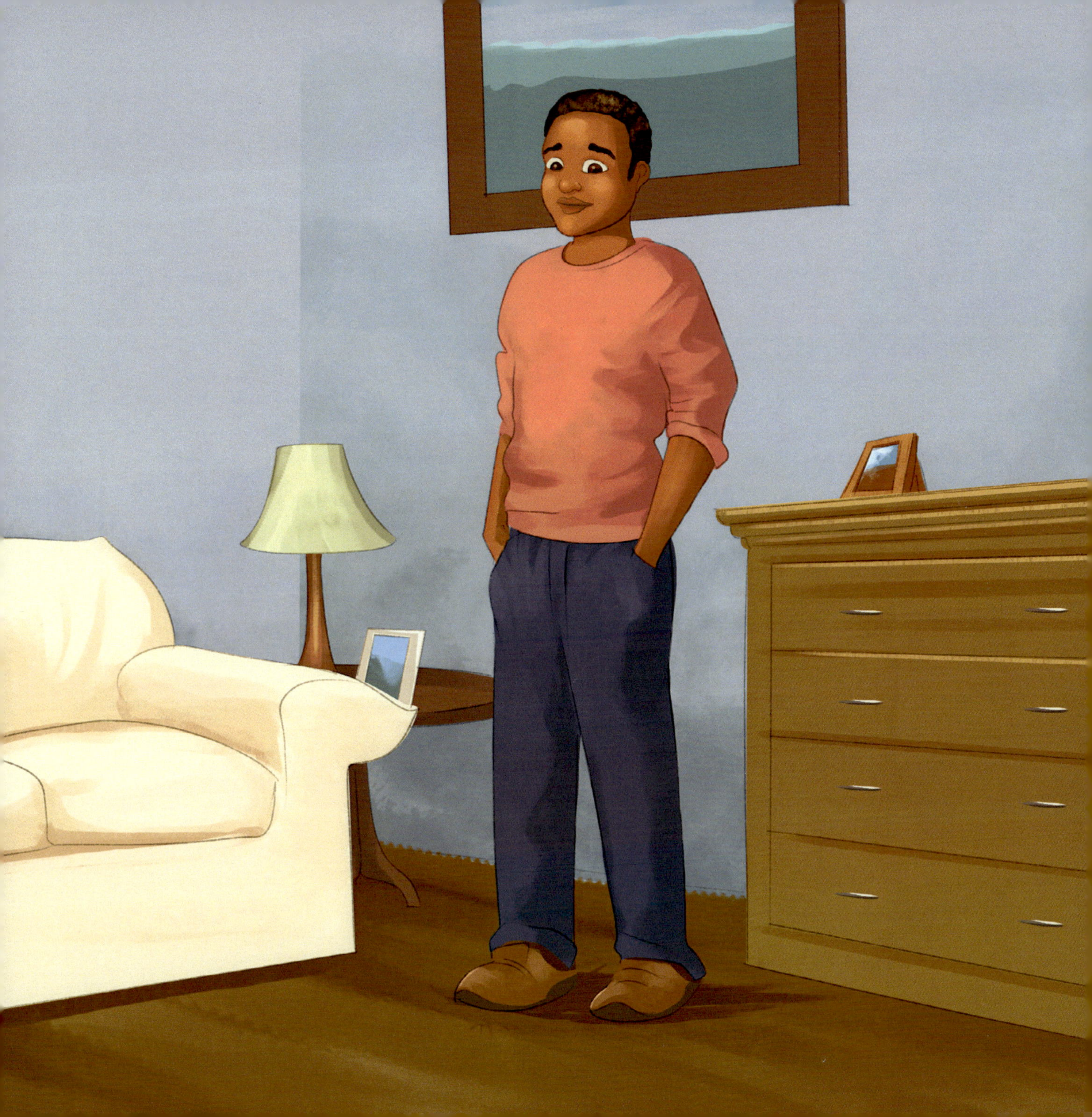

"Well, human beings have a pigment in their skin called melanin. If someone has just a little bit of melanin, their skin is light. The more melanin you have, the darker your skin. So, because we are all made differently, we all have different amounts of melanin. That means some people look like creamy coffee, some look like caramel, some look like vanilla ice cream, some look like fudge and some look like hot chocolate. On top of that, people can be every shade in between."

"So, *Baba*, how do you decide what colour you are?" asked Tanaka inquisitively.

"You don't. You're born the way you are and that depends on what shade your parents are. You're the same shade as your family, or somewhere in between if your parents are different colours. You see Uncle Taku and Auntie Lucy? He's black and she's white, so your cousins are somewhere in the middle. They got a lot of melanin from Uncle Taku and just a little from Auntie Lucy, so they ended up in the middle, like vanilla fudge."

"But, *Baba*, what about our cousin Tinemi? How come she has white skin and blonde hair but everyone else in her family has brown skin?" Tafara enquired.

"Well..." *Baba* was thinking of an answer, when *Gogo*, who was a retired nurse, stepped in.

"That's a good question and a very good observation, Tafara! We can explain Tinemi's skin colour through the study of genes. What you need to know now, though, is that when she was growing inside her mummy's womb, she didn't get any melanin from her father *or* her mother. She has albinism."

Ignoring the part about 'jeans', Tafara exclaimed, "Oh, I seeeee...!" as the penny dropped.

"You know what? I really like everybody looking different," Tanaka said.

"Yes, and we should never judge people or what they're capable of by the way they look. Nor should we treat them differently just because of their melanin concentration," *Baba* winked. "Now, girls, and, *Gogo*, you've done a sterling job on this patchwork blanket. We're all going to enjoy snuggling up in it for a long time. But *vasikana*, right now it's time to say goodbye to *Gogo* and *Khulu*."

They dutifully, but affectionately, said in unison, "*Murare zvakanaka, Gogo na Khulu,*" and melted in their hugs before heading next door, their heads buzzing with all this new-found knowledge.

Chapter 05

Just two minutes later, they were at their house, ready for their bedtime routine. Soon they'd finished their showers and brushed their teeth. Mama escorted them to their bedroom to tuck them into their duvets.

"Tafara, I remember when you were 3 years old and I left you with your bestie Rebecca and her family because I had to go to the hospital to give birth to your sister, Tanaka," she paused to let out a giggle. "Rebecca's mum gave all the kids a bath and she told me afterwards that Rebecca's big brother, Ron, who was only 4 or 5 then, was surprised and said to you, 'Oh, so your skin is black all over! I thought it was just your face and hands!' Aren't you little people funny?"

"Yes, Mama! We're absolutely hysterical!" replied Tanaka and everyone collapsed in giggles.

"Actually, that reminds me," Mama said as she remembered something she wanted to show the girls. She spun 'round and dashed next door for her laptop. When she returned, she squeezed herself in between the girls to show them one of her discoveries. Mama loved exploring anything and everything and sharing her finds.

"Girls. Look at these amazing pictures on Pinterest." Tafara loved Pinterest because it was full of exciting ideas and wonderful pictures. "This girl's name is April Star and she's a fashion model," said Mama as she pointed to the first one.

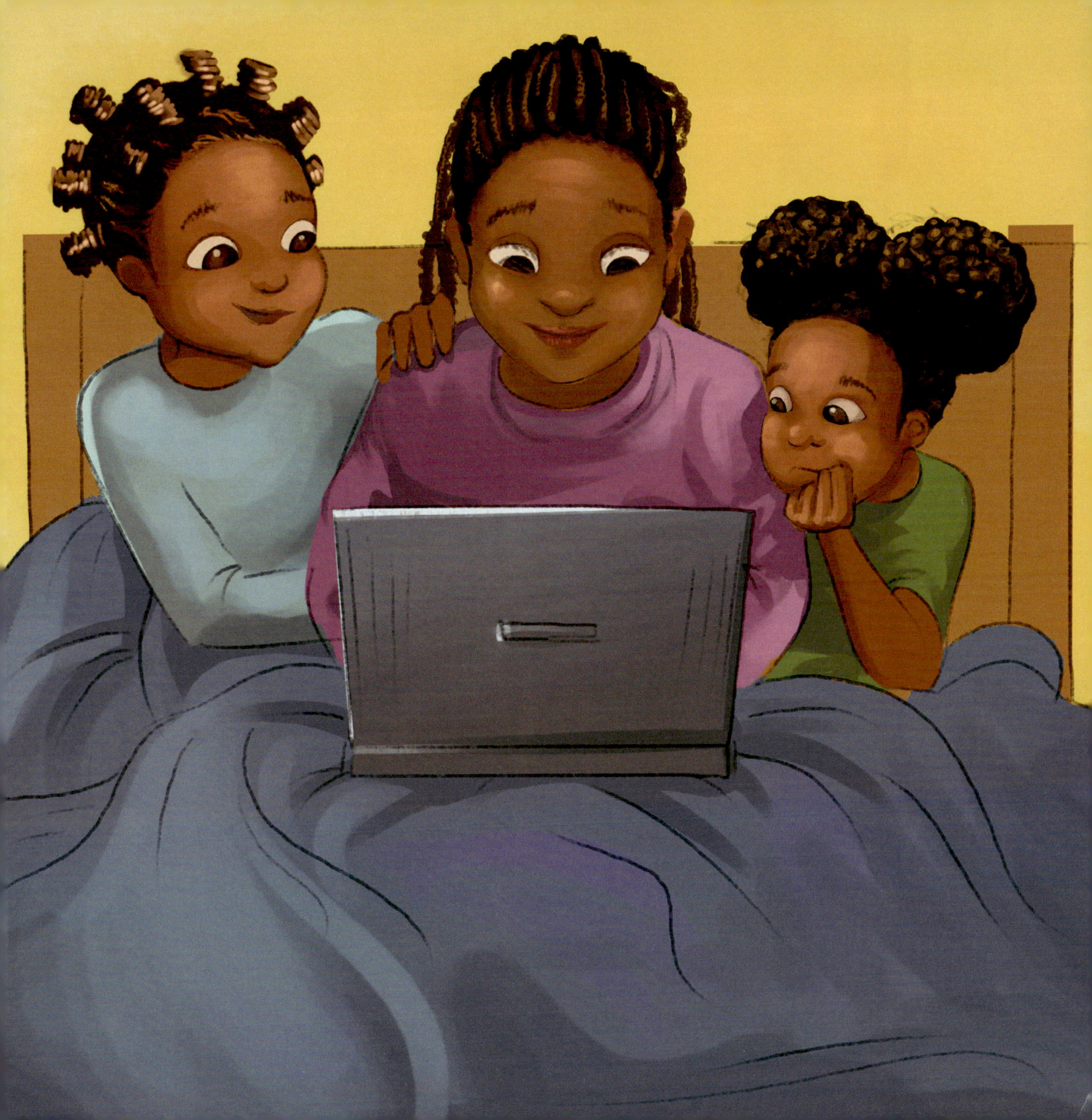

They studied the images. The girl in the pictures had patches of dark and light skin. They'd never seen anyone like that before! The pictures were beautiful! Tafara thought to herself, *I think Khulu would call these pictures 'artistic'.*

"Look, Mama. This one's a ballerina, like me!" Tafara excitedly read the caption underneath: "Michaela Mabinty DePrince, a Sierra Leonean-American ballerina."

"Why does she have those spots on her neck?" asked Tafara inquisitively.

"She has vitiligo," Mama replied gently, "which means she has melanin on some parts of her body and not on other parts."

Mama could see that Tafara and Tanaka were thinking about what she'd just told them.

"So, does that mean that when she was in her mummy's womb, her mummy splashed a bit of melanin here and there? Like I do sometimes when I'm painting, and I end up with a fun design?" asked Tanaka.

"Yes, Tanaka. You can say that," replied Mama slowly, in awe of Tanaka's creative thinking. "And remember, we talked about your cousin Tinemi who has albinism? Well, look at these pictures of Lara and Mara Bawar. They are young albino twins who are models in their country, Brazil. Fascinating, right?"

Tanaka and Tafara stared quietly at the pictures. Mama wondered if they needed more time to soak it all in.

Just then, Tafara declared, "So, anyone can really be what they want to be, whatever they look like. Well," she shrugged her shoulders, "like *Khulu* said, looks like I just have to carry on pointing my toes and keeping my back straight, if I want to be ballerina."

"And I have to carry on stretching those arms out if I want to be a swimmer," chimed in Tanaka.

Mama smiled. Her job was done! She kissed them on their foreheads, whispered a soft prayer, wished them goodnight, tucked the duvets in and switched off the light.

As Tafara drifted off to sleep, she thought about what wonderful things happened at *Gogo's* house...after all the time-tabled bits. What a day! What a revelation! And what a colourful world!

The End

Glossary

Baba – Father

Chii chamurikugadzira – What are you making?

Ehe – Yes (colloquial/slang)

Gogo – Grandmother

Khulu – Grandfather

Mamuka – You've woken up

Maswera sei? – How was your day?

Murare zvakanaka, Gogo na Khulu – Sleep well, *Gogo* and *Khulu*

Nda'a nda'a kutopedza – short for *Ndanga ndava kutopedza* – I had almost finished

Ndaswera kana maswerawo – loosely translated – I've had a good day if you have too

Sadza – ground maizemeal, usually from white maize (*chibage*), which is the staple food in Zimbabwe. Brown or greenish versions are made from grains such as sorghum or millet, which is considered to be healthier than maizemeal

Vasikana - Girls

Author's Note

I am aware that the world is not yet a true meritocracy but that is beyond the scope of this children's book. Melanin is a gift. We should not let the dearth of it, its deficiency, its abundance or its distribution define how we relate to each other or how we see ourselves. I proudly represent the more well-endowed variety of humans and I wouldn't have it any other way. I have friends and family represented in every square of the patchwork blanket, including in my ancestry. To me, the very ideas of racism and colourism are ludicrous, that people would deny others opportunity because of melanin concentration is nonsensical. I am not naïve enough to believe that this book will end all prejudice, but added to all the other voices, past, present and future, I believe we can all speak together and let our whispers become a shout.

Thank you for taking the time to read this book. I wish you love, joy, peace and happiness, with all my heart.